For Anna and Flora —M.H.

To my family: S.E., H.C., P.A., O.J. —E.O.

❧ALADDIN

An imprint of Simon & Schuster Children's Publishing Division | 1230 Avenue of the Americas, New York,
New York 10020 | First Aladdin hardcover edition April 2019 | Text copyright © 2018 by Morag Hood
Illustrations copyright © 2018 by Ella Okstad | Originally published in Great Britain in 2018 by Simon & Schuster UK Ltd
All rights reserved, including the right of reproduction in whole or in part in any form. | ALADDIN and related logo are
registered trademarks of Simon & Schuster, Inc. | For information about special discounts for bulk purchases,
please contact Simon & Schuster Special Sales at 1-866-506-1949 or business@simonandschuster.com.
The Simon & Schuster Speakers Bureau can bring authors to your live event. | For more information or to book an event
contact the Simon & Schuster Speakers Bureau at 1-866-248-3049 or visit our website at www.simonspeakers.com.
Manufactured in China | 1218 LEO | 2 4 6 8 10 9 7 5 3 1 | Library of Congress Control Number 2018930412
ISBN 9781534431614 (hc) | ISBN 9781534431621 (eBook)

Sophie Johnson,
UNICORN EXPERT

BY
MORAG HOOD and ELLA OKSTAD
ILLUSTRATED BY

ALADDIN

New York   London   Toronto   Sydney   New Delhi

UNICORN
FESTIVAL

My name is
Sophie Johnson,
and I live with
a **UNICORN**.

Well, not just one, actually.

I think I have **17** at the moment.

It can be hard work looking
after so many.

There is always a lot to do.

Luckily, I am a unicorn expert.

I am very busy teaching my unicorns everything they need to know.

We start with **magic**.

Then I show them how to hunt for food . . .

. . . and I teach them
about the dangers of . . .

BALLOONS!

Sometimes my unicorns lose their horns.

But I don't worry,

because they soon grow back.

Living with unicorns can be a bit tricky.

They are quite messy.

I try to explain that magic
is more important than mess,

but I don't think Mom understands.

Unicorns have many enemies,

so sometimes

I **have** to protect them.

Being a unicorn expert
is harder than you'd think.

Really, it's a good thing I'm here.

Some people don't even know
what a **REAL** unicorn looks like!

That's why they need me—
SOPHIE JOHNSON, Unicorn Expert.